The Galvanized Girl

THE RISE OF DELILAH DITCH

Nikki Nelson-Hicks

Third Crow Press Gallatin TN

Third Crow Press
640 Bradford Drive
Gallatin, TN 37066

Publisher's Note: This is a work of fiction. Names, characters, places, and incidents are a product of the author's imagination. Locales and public names are sometimes used for atmospheric purposes. Any resemblance to actual people, living or dead, or to businesses, companies, events, institutions, or locales is completely coincidental.

The Galvanized Girl/Nikki Nelson-Hicks. -- 1st ed.
ISBN 978-1-7320967-2-1

Come, you Spirits that tend on mortal thoughts, unsex me here...

- Lady Macbeth

"So, I jus' talk into this metal can here? And it remembers all what I say? Cor. Ain't that a spot of amazing or what?

"Okay, so, my best girl, Aggie, set up this contraption so it could capture my side of the story and others could hear it and judge it for theirselves.

"So, here it is. Listen close 'cause I ain't telling it again.

"My name is Delilah Ditch but most people know me as The Galvanized Girl. I want to set down the record straight, before God and this electrified tin can; I never aimed to kill nobody, much less start a war..."

CHAPTER ONE

Pryde and the Angels

In the middle of London, on a busy middle-class street, there was a row of typical middle-class townhouses wedged between other middle-class townhouses.

But only one townhouse had Angels.

As you walked through the foyer, past the parlour and into the kitchen, you'd find a double locked door. Behind it, a flight of stairs led down to the basement where another door, triple locked, opened to two rooms. One room was an operating laboratory, a place of metal slabs, bubbling chemicals and the spectacle of lightning dancing between gleaming silver balls.

Adjacent to it was a white, serene room where concentric circles of gold were etched into the floor to summon the voices of Angels.

This was a hidden place, here in this middle-class neighborhood, where Science and Magic came together and forged an alliance to ensure the future glory of England.

And the whole affair hung heavily on the shoulders of Dr. Thaddeus Pryde, a little man in a poorly made wig.

Tonight, Dr. Pryde pounded his fists against his forehead as he walked the concentric golden circles like a monk in a labyrinth. Some nights their voices filled his head with ease. Other nights, like tonight, it took a little more finesse and tweaking. He made a mental note to see if astrological configurations might be the key to achieving an optimal signal.

However, as for now, matters would need to be handled in a fleshier direction.

He pulled off his wig. Across his scalp, like a copper crown, there were three circular dials. It was an ancient form of trepanning he had taken one step further. The holes were kept open by brass rings. Each ring had a dilating cover that he could, by twisting the dials, control the aperture and attune himself to the Angels' signals.

He pulled out a strap of leather he kept in his pocket and bit down. Turning the dials exacerbated the infected pustules that plagued his scalp. His teeth ground into the leather and he muffled his screams. It was a torture he would gladly endure to protect England from the Angel's prophesied devastating Coming War.

DING-DING-DING

Yes! First, the bells and then the purifying, cold static rush that flooded his brain making his eyeballs itch. He had made connection!

"IS IT DONE?" The voice burned through his mind. "DO YOU HAVE THE FINAL SOLDIER?"

He pulled the strap out of his mouth and wiped the blood from his forehead. "Yes, my Angels, yes! I have it here! The first prototype of a galvanized exoskeleton with neural inlaid uplinks just as your blessed diagrams bade me to create. I only need now a human subject with which to test it."

"THEN IT IS NOT DONE. FIND A SUBJECT. TIME IS GROWING SHORT. THE WAR WILL BE UPON ENGLAND

AND YOU WILL NOT BE READY. ALL WILL PERISH. FINISH AND YOUR REWARDS WILL BE TEN THOUSAND FOLD."

"Yes…yes!" He pleaded. "I wish only to do your bidding but, my Angels, I need-"

There was the sharp electric snap that seared through his scalp and the link was cut.

The little man growled in frustration. They do this every time! Commands and promises of rewards but no inkling as to how to complete the task!

He stomped over to the laboratory next to the Summoning Room and stared up in awe at the Galvanized Exoskeleton. The Angels instructed him how to put it together, piece by piece. They foretold of a war that was brewing and that this suit, the Final Soldier, would be worn by England's fighting men and bring them to victory.

It was a beautiful thing, this skeleton of silver filigree. It was only a prototype, a first draft. The finished product would be like a knight's armor, solid and whole. It would be a thing to fill the hearts and minds of

England's enemies with terror. If only he could finish it!

For months, Pryde had experimented with a modified exoskeleton by crippling street dogs he bought from a local rat catcher. He would separate the spinal column at different vertebra, snipping nerves here and there, the usual sort of medical hijinks, until he was satisfied with the paralysis. Then he would weld the animals into modified dog sized galvanized suits. None of the dogs survived very long after the procedure but each experiment brought him closer and closer to success.

The next step was obvious. He would have to test the protype on a human subject. It would need a strong constitution to be able to survive the surgical neural couplings and be of considerable stature to carry the weight of the suit, the way a beetle carries its own skeleton on its back.

But the empty slab in the center of his laboratory mocked him.

"Even a cripple would be better than nothing, if only to test out the neural relays," he said to himself as he closed the valves on his scalp and readjusted the wig on his head.

He walked up the stairs to the upper rooms and double locked the door that led to his basement laboratory. If only the Angels would give him a sign, something to reassure him that all would be well.

"That's the problem with spirits. No sense of decorum." He straightened his tie and checked in the mirror that his face was clean. He fussed with the wig and flattened it to his head the best he could. "Buck up, old chum," he said to his reflection. "The Lord will provide. England will not fall, no, not while we are on watch."

He took a deep breath, plastered a welcoming smile on his face and lifted the dark green shade on his front door window to show to the world that the office of Doctor Thaddeus Pryde, Surgeon, was open for practice.

"Say something about me? Well, there's not much to talk about before I was the Galvanized Girl. But, if that's what you want, Aggie, that's what I'll do.

"I was raised on porridge and a strap at the Starkwater Foundling Home over in the East End. The heartbroke git in charge of naming burdened me with the tag of Delilah. Not that I should piss and moan too much; at least he went Biblical on me. It weren't so lucky for the three girls that came in earlier. Ambergris and Bursa paid the price for the medical dictionary someone dropped off in the bin. You don't even want to know what the third girl was saddled with.

"It's a tradition probably thought up by some goody-goods in the West End over some social tea to make our surnames come from the place where we was found. Like 'Abbey' for some unwanted bastard left at a church, see? They found me, a fat, red-headed babe, abandoned and squalling in a ditch and, well, there you go. I was tagged

for life as Deliliah Ditch. Life's a right joke, really.

"There wasn't much schoolin' done at the Home. Not much call for it, really. None of our lot was destined to be anything other than cogs to be used until our teeth ground down and then tossed out with the garbage. What? Did that get your britches up your crack, Miss College Girl? I'm sorry to be blunt, Aggs, but I'm just saying what is my truth. That is what you want, innit? That's what this all about, right? Right. So... those that weren't lucky enough to get homes were all set up with jobs in the local factories. Because I've always been more draught horse than a trembling doe like that poor girl, Chlamydia, I got set up working with the power looms over at the mill. I moved heavy machinery around and kept things in line. It was a good job for what it was and nobody never bothered me. I was even able to scrape up a little bit of savings. I had plans back then. Don't laugh. Everybody has dreams, even us throwaways. I figured I'd work and get up enough money to start something of my own, be my own person someday. And things were happening; things were slowly turning my way until the day it all went to hell."

ILLUSTRATED TIMES, LONDON ISSUE
March 1897
TRAGIC LOSS OF LIFE AND HORRIFIC INJURIES
Mechanized Looms kill unfortunate workers

Mr. Wilfred K. Stoggs, disgraced owner of Stoggs Mill and Power Looms Company, Deacon Street, London is in Old Bailey, charged with the senseless deaths of twelve young girls and women.

The hellish conditions suffered by the employees of Stoggs, mainly young girls and women from the workhouse, were revealed after a pack of feral dogs chasing a rat, rampaged through the building causing the mechanized loom machines that were packed in two dozen to a floor, well above posted safety regulations, to fall over like a stack of dominoes, crushing and maiming all the employees in its path.

Dr. Thaddeus Pryde, a local surgeon, generously lent a helping hand to the victims of the Stoggs' Loom Tragedy last week by personally escorting them, one by one, to the local charity hospital.

'He is an inspiration. He even took upon himself to take the dead to the morgue.' a reporter quoted a nurse. 'No families, no one to claim them. Poor souls will probably end up in Potter's Field. He is truly a paragon of English virtue.'

"I did all I could under the circumstances." The good doctor said as he helped to cart the injured and the dead to hospital. "The rest is in God's hands."

"There was this girl, Jill, skittery little thing, scared of her own shadow. She had a mangled hand, so we gave her pennies to do little odd jobs. When the dogs rushed in, she got scared and run underneath the looms. I went in to fetch her, but it was all knackered. One of the looms toppled and squashed her like a bug. As God as my witness, I tried to get that damn thing off her, but another loom fell, right on my neck.

"The last thing I remember was a man in thick glasses with black, stiff hair, licking his lips and saying, 'God provides, yes, He does.'

"He held a sweet-smelling rag over me nose and mouth until everything went black. When I woke up, there wasn't much of Delilah left.

"I was the Galvanized Girl."

CHAPTER TWO

God Save The Queen

Dr. Thaddeus Pryde was not a religious man. While he had never crossed the line of atheism, he had dragged his foot through it a time or two.

That was before the Angels.

He was barely thirty when they first spoke to him. The voices filled him with equations, knowledge, and visions of a horrific future war where people fought in ditches and the air was poison. The visions that poured into his brain were hellish and caused his body to seize as if every muscle was in vise.

His father, a dedicated and respected physician, immediately sent his son to the country for a fresh air treatment.

When Thaddeus returned home, he confronted his father and told him about the visions, the Angels and how he, Thaddeus Pryde, had been given a task to save his Queen and county.

His father's response was to ship him off to another retreat.

The water peddlers at the health spa tried to convince him that he was suffering from delusions and psychotic hallucinations. Pills for melancholia were forced down his throat and, for a while, his mind was calm again. The Voices were still. Pryde was on the verge of giving in to the physician's diagnosis when the Angels woke him from his sleep, warning him of a fire that was to consume the entire building. He fled, taking with him only his notebooks and hid in the forest. Within an hour, a lightning bolt struck the building and sparked a fire that consumed everything. He was the only survivor. All those that had opposed and doubted his Angels were lost to the flames. After that, his devotion became absolute. The Angels taught him how to create the Concentric Circle Grid, to cut and drill holes in his skull to allow for better connectivity, instructed him in all the mysteries of galvanism, and chose him to be the Saviour of Great Britain.

Dr. Pryde stood outside his basement laboratory, bowed his head and mumbled a prayer. "I thank thee, Oh Lord of Lords, Hosts of Hosts, and Creator of all Things, for this gift. The Lord provides, oh yes. Hallelujah, praises unto Your Name. Amen."

Inside, his assistant, Agnes Walter, was preparing for the operation. She was his sister's daughter; Pryde couldn't bring himself to think of her as a niece. She was 'Maria's daughter' or 'Girl' nothing else. The Girl was a headstrong thing, too much like her German father, and graduated college the past year. Pryde shook his head at the idea. A girl with a degree! What a waste of paper. Nevertheless, she knew her way around a laboratory and worked for nothing. "God provides." Pryde muttered and sighed. "It's not for me to second guess."

He unlocked the laboratory door and walked inside. There it was! The prototype that would save England and the lucky subject that would be the first to inhabit it. He marveled over the sight on the operating table. God had provided a marvelous specimen, indeed! Tall, strong and would survive the operation. Probably. He calculated quickly and nodded. Yes, very probably. Pryde stopped and silently made a prayer of thanks and stepped into the room.

"Girl! Have you finished the preparations?"

Aggie was whispering to the subject and stroking its head. "Yes, Uncle Thad. I have shaved and-"

"NO!" Pryde stomped over to her and pulled a leather strap from his pocket. "You are to call me DOCTOR Pryde. How many times do I need to remind you?" He slapped her across the back three times with the rough leather; Agnes turned away but did not cry out. "How many times before you get it into your thick, stupid girl head?"

"Apologies, *Doctor* Uncle Pryde."

He raised the strap but let it drop. "Oh, what's the use? No, wait! Shaved? Completely?"

"Yes."

"Then," he asked, pointing with a trembling finger, "what is that?"

"That small patch? The schematic doesn't go anywhere close to the pubis and surely, Uncle, we can give her some small piece of privacy?"

"No, it must be clean! All of it!" He clenched his eyes and stomped down his foot with each word. "CLEAN, CLEAN, CLEAN! It must be clean!"

"So be it. It won't take a minute."

Pryde opened his eyes and it was as if it were the first time he saw the woman on the slab. Her skin was flawless, like porcelain. Her breasts were large, and the rose-pink nipples hardened as the razor scraped away at the groin. Suddenly, a flush of desire that flooded his brain, drained down his spine but was stopped dead at his crotch. Years ago, with just a few swipes of a sharp scalpel, Dr. Thaddeus Pryde had removed the frailty of human lust from his person. He took a deep breath and smiled as the feeling faded away.

"There." Agnes wiped the razor on her thigh. "Happy now?"

"Oh, yes. Very. Let's begin. Bring the voice recording device closer. But be careful! This surgery needs to be chronicled for posterity."

"Yes, Unc- Doctor."

Agnes rolled a cart over near the operating table and locked the wheels into place. On the cart was a recording device that Pryde had devised from the mysterious schematics sent to him from the Angels. It was a metal box with wheels that wound brown tape that caught the words from thin air. It was a miraculous marvel just one of the many visions the Angels poured into his brain.

He pushed down a button and the wheels turned.

"The date is October 19, in the Year of our Lord, 1898. Doctor Thaddeus Pryde officiating. Assisting me is Agnes Walter."

"Doctor Agnes Walter." The Girl corrected.

"I stand corrected. The recently graduated and not yet tested, *Doctor* Agnes Walter, assisting.

"The subject in today's operation is a young female, early twenties, 6'1" and weighs approximately 11 stone. Very healthy complexion. Musculature is sturdy and robust. A fracture of the cervical vertebrate paralyzed the subject from the shoulders down, immobilizing the subject completely. However, the viability of the subject's pain receptors were verified by the discomfort caused when repeatedly jabbed with needles over the length of the body.

"The subject is conscious and by the darting of the eyes, seemingly aware. Brain functions appear moderately normal.

"The purpose for this operation is to repair the subject's immobility by bypassing the damaged nervous system with a neural exoskeleton that will not only give the subject mobility but an array of other abilities that, I am assured, are necessary for the salvation of Her Majesty's Empire.

"God save the Queen."

"Anesthesia has been administered." Agnes said. "She is asleep and life signs appear normal."

"Then let us begin…"

"What I miss most are my tits.

"Floyd Candle used to say they were 'pillows for the gods'. What? Oh, don't blush, Aggs. Christ on a stick, I'm not some blushing rose of England; that petal was plucked long ago before I'd even reached my prime plucking age. Poor old sod. His name was Rodney Staggs. I hear he goes for boys these days which explains a lot now that I think about it. You might have seen him. He sells his wares, if you get my meaning, down near the docks. I used to wave to him now and then on the way to the factory. He had a killer eye for hosiery and lingerie. Give that boy a load of satin and a sewing machine and he could make you anything.

"What? Oh, yeah...sorry. I was woolgathering, memories taking me away to when I was all me, good old Delilah Ditch,

through and through. Sorry I can't say that for much else of me.

"Anyway, my tits. Christ Above, they were glorious things, truly they were, but not to the Doc. No, they ruined the 'line of the form' or some such cockrot. He tore at them something fierce, barely leaving enough to cram inside a tuzzie-muzzie.

"Stop blushing, Aggie. Christ alive, girl. Get your nose out of a book once in a while.

"But I ain't discounting what the doc did for me. No! First off, he did fix me back. I wasn't crippled no more. The exo-whatsit-skeleton moved with me and I could move because of it. I don't understand the learning behind it. You'd have to go to Aggs for all of that mess. She's tried to explain it to me but the words just jumble up inside me head until I feel like I'm gonna burst. Still, in the end, all that matters is that I could walk and, better than that, I could fly! I gots these metal round discs in me palms and also in the bottoms of me feet. All I have to do is push down and up I go! Something to do with magnets and the Earth, I dunno the reasoning behind it but it is a right nipple tweaking thrill, I am here to tell you! I can't

do it for long, just in short bursts, it knackers me out something awful.

"It's easier to use my palm bits to pull or push things. That barely tires me out at all. Best thing is that I'll never have to get up to get a pint at the pub ever again. Just pull and presto! The glass is in me hand! It is brilliant, I'm here to tell you.

"Of course, it weren't all fun and games. Not when it came to the Doc. He put me through drills and exercised me till I thought my heart would burst out of me chest. I needed to work extra hard to keep strong so's I could work with the exo-skeleton and not just be controlled by it, see? Still, I had a few fun times, whenever I could get away from the doc. I liked to sneak away and fly, late at night, what with the streets being dark and empty, I figgered I wouldn't be seen, right? Goes to show you how stupid I am. The doc knew. He had been tracking me like a hunter, all those nights. That was how I learned the hard way that he had a kill switch. He could turn me off whenever he liked. He'd warned me about wearing down me batteries and once he caught me playing, pushing myself up as high as I could go, ya know, just playing and flexing my muscles. Next thing I know, my body locks up, like I

am frozen up, right? And I fell to the ground. After I crashed, he stood over me and just leered at me, getting off on watching me struggle just to breathe."

"Remember this, Girl," he said, "If I flip this switch, the frame holding your broken carcass together turns off and so do you. Do you fully grasp that? Outside this metal frame, you are nothing, do you understand? I own you. You are MINE."

"I have never been so scared in all my life. I knew by the way he stared down at me, his eyes like dark slits, I knew then, I weren't nothing more to him than a kid's wind up soldier. And he were the bad kind of kid, the one that likes nothing more than to twist."

CHAPTER THREE

The Girl Unveiled

ILLUSTRATED TIMES, LONDON ISSUE

April 1898

THE GLORIOUS GALVANIZED GIRL!!

*Scientific Breakthrough of the Century!
*Manmade Flight Within Our Lifetime!
*A Heroine for Children! Galvanized Girl
costumes flying off the shelves!
*Religious Groups Are Asking: Is The
Galvanized Girl an Abomination?*

After a two-week run of sold out performances, Doctor Thaddeus Pryde is taking his creation to see the Queen and some of her honoured guests.

"I am honoured, of course." said Dr. Pryde. "It is the highest compliment Her Majesty can bestow on a loyal subject."

The Galvanized Girl has become a showstopper and beloved icon of London's children.

"She's fantastic!" Majorie, age 6, in a silver cape and hat to mimic her hero, said after a Saturday matinee. "The way she flies

and when she pulls metal balls off shelves and throws them around! It's like agic!"

And the illusion of magic is what has religious groups in the area concerned. Reverent Snoot has published a pamphlet which he hands out after each performance.

The pamphlet states: 'Ignoring the vulgarity of the costume, the idea of human flight flies, pardon the wordplay, in the face of God. We are children of dust and it is on the ground we should stay!'

Reverend Snoot declined to comment any further.

Local scientists also have concerns but more of an earthier nature.

"Dr. Pryde has refused to allow any of our colleagues to examine the schematics of the exoskeleton suit." Professor Harrison of the Royal Society of Physicians, Engineers and Scientists said, "Nor will he share with us the technology or means of energizing the suit. With all respect, Dr. Pryde is only a surgeon. It is a matter of public safety that new technology should be carefully vetted by those gentlemen with the proper accreditation."

When addressed with these concerns, Dr. Pryde merely said, "God provides and protects his chosen."

Despite the controversy being stirred up by the religious and scientific communities, it is the public's hearts and minds that The Galvanized Girl has taken root.

"Damifino what the eggheads or Bible thumpers are on about." quipped Robert Howard, dockhand, 32 Lantern's Way. "That flyin' chuckaboo is bang up to the elephant as far as I can see! Fart ripping good show!"

We here at the Illustrated Times hope Her Majesty feels the same.

"Doc wasn't as much of a seamstress as a surgeon. He had a devil of a time stitching me into an angel suit. And that bloody wig! Itched something fierce against me own stubble. He had a collection of wigs, he did. Not that I asked questions, not my place to. I figgered he had a bald wife."

CHAPTER FOUR

The Angels

When the Angels spoke to him outside the Summoning Room, it was sudden and vicious, like a lightning bolt of raw, electric fire burning through his skull. Dr. Pryde fell to his knees and crawled towards the golden circles. He fished out the leather strap his kept in his pocket and bit down as he clawed the wig off to adjust the apertures of the dials on his head.

"Yes, my Angels?" The pain eased as he got closer to the center of the circles. "You called?"

"WHY HAVEN'T YOU CONTACTED THE MINISTRY OF DEFENSE?"

"What ministry is this? I am unfamiliar with this denomination."

There was a muttering between the Angels.

"UM...WE MEAN THE WAR OFFICE."

"Yes! It is part of the plan! Her Majesty's curiosity has been whetted and I have been granted an audience. I promise you! None of this is to further me! It is all for your glory!"

"SERIOUSLY? YOU WILL BE PRESENTING THE PROTOTYPE TO QUEEN VICTORIA? IN PERSON?"

"Yes! She has invited many important heads of State to attend the event. She wants to dazzle our allies and rivals. After that we can-"

"WAIT....ARE YOU SAYING THE KAISER BE THERE? WILHEIM II OF GERMANY. HE WILL BE THERE?"

"Yes, I believe so. He is the Queen's favorite grandson."

"EXCELLENT! OH, HOLY CRAP! THIS IS BETTER THAN WE HAD HOPED FOR! MAYBE....OH, THE KAISER! IN OUR SIGHTS! THERE DOESN'T NEED TO BE A WAR AT ALL! EXCELLENT!"

Another voice chimed in.

"WAIT, GARY, WE DON'T KNOW HOW IT WILL AFFECT THE UPLINKS. ONCE IT IS DONE, IT COULD KILL HER."

"BUT WE HAVE A SHOT AT AVOIDING WORLD WAR I! THAT'S WHAT ALL THIS IS ABOUT, RIGHT, HAROLD? NO WORLD WAR I AND THEN NO WORLD WAR II. IMAGINE IT."

"YEAH…."

"PRYDE, WE ARE DOWNLOADING THE NEW SCHEMATICS THAT WILL INCREASE THE POWER OF THE SUIT. DO EXACTLY AS YOU ARE TOLD."

Dr. Thaddeus Pryde crumpled to the ground, blood dripping from his ears. He fell over and curled into a fetal position, his face in a silent scream as he gripped the sides of his head, fighting to keep it from exploding.

From the shadows, there were two very earthly eyes watching and attached to them a very scared woman wondering what the ever-loving hell was happening to her uncle.

"Hello.

"My name is Doctor Agnes Walter and I wanted to state for the record that I had no idea of his, my uncle, that is, Dr. Thaddeus Pryde, of his militaristic intentions. When I agreed to work with him, my mother said he was designing a way to help the crippled. I'm an engineer and, as a woman, was desperate for any kind of experience, to prove my worth despite my femininity. I believed that was what we were working on until the night I walked into his private study. I know I shouldn't have but I heard such strange, horrible voices. It was like a hive of bees, a strange static hum. It put my teeth on edge. My curiosity got the better of me. If only I had had the courage to stop him. Perhaps Edgar would still be here.

"God, I am pathetic. I am so sorry, Edgar.

"*I knew! Goddammit, I knew by looking at the schematics, at the power lines, I knew it wouldn't work! It was madness to think you could pump that sort of raw electric power through simple neural synapses. But I didn't trust myself. That is my fault, not Delilah's, not even Uncle Thad's. I should have stopped it. Their blood is on my hands. All of those people in the park. And my dear Edgar. I should never have brought you into this catastrophe. If I had only...but it doesn't matter now.*

"*They are all dead. There is no way to bring them back. Delilah and I are doing all we can to make up for it.*

"*And, from the bottom of my heart, I am sorry. So very, very sorry.*"

Excerpt from the Journal of Queen Victoria

....beef tips and roast potatoes were served. The manners of my grandson, Wilheim, towards his uncle, the Prince of Wales, were as contentious as usual. The terrible, hurtful words that he spews out. It is shameful and unbecoming. I am saddened that his succession to the German throne has done nothing to temper his feisty temper. I shall have a talk with Vicky about his behaviour.

On a happier note, tomorrow is the royal unveiling of one of Britain's most ambitious glories, The Galvanized Girl! A royal subject that flies! She is the sole reason I invited Wilheim to spend the weekend, even though he insisted on bringing with him a veritable platoon of Germans that hang on his every word. I wanted to impress him with one of Britain's scientific advances.   I hope this wonderful sight will soften his hard heart towards his homeland.

Oh! And lest I forget the wonderful gifts bestowed upon us by Dr. Thaddeus Pryde, the creator of the Galvanized Girl. He gave me a lovely silver angel brooch. For the men, he presented them with silver winged medallions. I know that Willie will enjoy his immensely. He has such a lust for military brouhaha.

ILLUSTRATED TIMES, LONDON ISSUE
April 1898
THE KAISER TAKES POTSHOTS AT THE ROYAL SWANS

Foreign Affairs Office Attempts to Unruffle Feathers with Raffle for Locals to Attend the Royal Viewing of the Galvanized Girl.

There was much public outcry against Queen Victoria's grandson, Wilheim, the German Emperor, this week when he and a group of his foreign cronies took potshots at the royal swans swimming in the Thames. Three swans died, two suffered broken wings and a nest of eggs were trampled by persons unknown.

The Kaiser's State Secretary for Foreign Affairs, Bernard von Bulow, to salvage the situation, has partnered with the Illustrated Times to raffle off three tickets to see Galvanized Girl perform exclusively for the Queen.

The winners are Mrs. George Torrance, Mr. Reginald Fowlkes and Thomas Fielding, a towheaded, 9-year-old son of a grocer. He was also gifted with a medal from the Kaiser which the little boy wore with pride.

The Queen was unavailable for comment.

"Doc didn't say much to me about what he was doing. Not that I would've understand a hair of it anyways. He just asked me to come into the lab for a tune-up. That's what he called them: tune-ups. Just tinkering around with some of the relay whatsits in my back. Done it a million times. I stripped down to nothing and got up on the slab. It was a new one I ain't never seen before, shaped out like a big X. I situated myself the best I could. Then he strapped my legs, upper arms and chest down tight with leather straps. Lucky for me, I'm not a modest girl

Still, I shoulda known then this was something more than another a 'tune-up'."

CHAPTER FIVE

An Important Date

In a secret room, at the bottom of middle class townhouse, wedged between two other middle classed townhouses, the mad, obsessed, and brilliant, Dr. Thaddeus Pryde cut away the flesh of the prototype's fingers, palm, and forearm, folding back the skin like a curtain. He inserted the slim, silver coated endo-skeletal rods and laid a squishy mesh coating over it before peeling the skin back into place and sewing it close.

Dr. Pryde worked like a man possessed. He shucked off his coat and blouse and was clad in only tan, wrinkled pants and a blood splattered white undershirt. He left the wig on a hook in the Summoning Room. The matted plate of hair interfered with the Angels and, worst of all, it itched like the devil.

He scratched at the irritated pustules until blood and pus streaked down his scalp and stained his neckline. He wiped his neck with a handkerchief as he finished transcribing the operation into the recorder.

"I have switched off the neural inlays in the subject to affect a kind of paralysis and pseudo-aesthetic in preparation for the surgery. As the Angels have instructed, in the left arm, I have overlaid the endoskeleton over the subject's natural bone, cushioned it with the surgical mesh given to me by the Angels and sewn the injury closed.

"I inserted next to the resistor pad a coil device into the palm and forearm of the right arm. I inserted the small silver energized sphere into the subject's left palm.

"Respiration and heart rate of the subject are elevated but not critical.

"I shall activate the coil and test the device in…three…two…."

Before Pryde finished the countdown, the door opened to reveal Agnes, her mouth gaping like a small bass. Behind her stood a strange man in a gray colored suit.

"UNCLE!" Agnes shouted, "What in the name of God-"

"ONE!"

Thaddeus Pryde pushed a shiny red button. The room shook with a sharp crack and a fiery snap as the Galvanized Girl was enveloped in a ball of lightning. The metal platform shook as her naked body arched and undulated, kept down only by the force of the leather straps. Lightning hopped from each fingertip and pooled in the center of her palms into swirling, rainbow colored plasma balls.

"Uncle! My God, what have you done? Poor Deliliah!" Agnes moved towards her friend but the man in the gray suit pulled her back.

"Don't be a fool! You'll be electrocuted!"

"Electrocuted? Don't be absurd!" Pryde pushed the button again and the light show popped out of existence.

"Delilah!" Agnes ran to her friend and quickly checked her vital signs. She nodded at her companion and began undoing the leather straps.

"Let the record show," Pryde shouted to the voice recorder, "the experiment was interrupted by Agnes Walter, my former assistant who is henceforth now sacked, and an unknown busybody in a gray suit! Give me your name so I can put it on record before I throw you both out of here!"

"I am Dr. Edgar Harrison of the Royal Society of Physicians, Engineers and Scientists."

"Ha! A spy, no doubt! I always knew one of you ivy towered weasels would come to steal my work!"

"No, sir, no. I am not here to steal from you. I'm here to help you. Agnes…I mean, Dr. Walter asked me to come to see about your health. While I am quite curious as to whatever natural mystery you have uncovered, I can see by your physical sate that the toll for such a discovery is too much for one human to bear. Please let me help you."

"Toll? What do you persnickety, dried up academic farts know about toll? It's all jealousy! Jealousy. I was the one chosen! Not you! Me! A simple surgeon. And why? Because I am not afraid to get my hands bloodied or feel sweat on my brow. I was the one who sacrificed bone and blood all for the sake of completing the Great Project!"

"I am but a simple physician myself, sir. I specialize in mind theory." Dr. Harrison smiled softly and took a step forward. "Although, I admit, I am quite beside myself just looking at your work. Help me to understand. What are you doing to this girl and what, if I may be so bold, in the name of Heaven, have you done to yourself?"

Pryde tapped at the brass rings in his scalp. "Ah, quite an apropos invocation, Dr. Harrison."

Another step, close enough now to touch him. "What do you mean?"

"For, in the name of Heaven, certain adjustments to this mortal shell had to be made. Sacrifices offered and tortures endured. All in the name of Heaven and for the safety of England."

Dr. Harrison took Pryde by the arm. "Please, sir, let me take you to a hospital."

"Hospital! HA! Asylum, more like! I won't go back there!"

Pryde brandished a scalpel, grabbed the doctor by the shoulder and pulled him close, digging the blade deeper into the man's gut as he pushed Harrison out of the laboratory, leading him to the Summoning Room.

Pryde whispered into the dying man's ear. "The Angels will not be denied! England will be saved and I will be remembered as her savior!"

Harrison fell inside the room with a thud and lied motionless.

Dr. Pryde turned his attentions towards his niece.

Agnes was so focused on the leather straps that she did not notice that her uncle was behind her until he put the bloodied scalpel under her chin.

"Leave it. Come with me." Pryde scraped the blade across her neck. No skin was broken but the threat was enough to make Agnes gasp. "Now, march like a good little soldier, yes, that's it. One foot in front of the other. That's right. Follow in the footsteps of your gentleman spy. And....IN YOU GO!"

Pryde pushed Agnes through the door, tripping her as she went so that she fell to her knees.

"Edgar!" she screamed at the sight of Dr. Harrison bleeding and unconscious. "Please, Uncle! Don't leave us! He'll die!"

"I'm quite booked up today, my dear. I have a very important date with the Queen. Next time, make an appointment!" Dr. Thaddeus Pryde sneered as he slammed the door and locked it.

"How did it feel? It's hard to describe.

"You ever been locked outside in winter, thin soles on your shoes wrapped in a coat that is a coat in name only? You know how the wind rakes away any bit of warmth your body can shiver out?

"Now, imagine dunking your frozen bones into a hot, steamy tub of water.

"Hurts like hell at first, like your nerves are waking up, on fire and screamin', but, after a bit, it feels really good. Damn good. Like you had no idea how cold and dead you were until you were boiled alive? Kinda like that.

"Does that make any sense?"

CHAPTER SIX

In Her Arms

"This doesn't make any sense."

Agnes ruffled through the dozens of journals she found on the bookcase. Some of the writing started out as legible, even if it was full of gibberish words like 'Tesla', 'String Theory' and 'Dimensional Continuum Relay', only to regress into scribbles and what looked like doodles.

"Let me see." Dr. Harrison pulled himself up, holding his gut and grimacing.

"Don't!" Agnes helped her friend up. "You are hurt."

"It's not as bad as all that, barely a puncture." Dr. Harrison smiled weakly at Agnes. "Something to say for wearing formal attire in spite of what the younger set thinks."

"You're not old, Edgar."

"Your affection has blinded you" He kissed her on her head, ruffling her honey blonde hair. "Now, show me what you found while I, um, was resting."

"Well, just look around you. My uncle has obviously gone completely insane. I couldn't make heads or tails of the markings carved into the gold inlays on the floor…"

"Aramaic."

"What?"

"The writing inside the circles. It's Aramaic. I recognize a few words, 'God', 'Saviour', 'Heaven' but that is all. Sorry, my ancient dead languages are rusty."

"You did better than me. Still, I found these journals. Sick or not, my uncle is a scientist and mad for note taking. See all these journals here? These are filled with plans we used when we first constructed the exoskeleton for Delilah."

"Why did she need one in the first place?"

"A horrible accident. She was paralyzed from the neck down and would have perished if not for the surgery."

"Did you question him as to where he received this technology?"

Agnes blushed. "No. I didn't want to anger him. I'm sorry, Edgar."

"But you are an engineer, not a surgeon," he said.

"I was convinced that this is the blending of two separate sciences. The future of a whole new branch, can you imagine that? I couldn't resist. I was desperate and needed to take anything I could to get experience. No one would take a woman on as an assistant."

"I understand, Agnes, truly I do. Scaling the walls of Academia as an alienist is just as treacherous."

"I found these journals, written just recently." A stack of leather bound books, seven deep, sat on the table. "I've only gone through a few but these schematics are nothing like the ones he showed me when we worked together. I can't make heads or tails out of them. I have no idea what this is about or what he is planning."

"Well then, let's turn to the last page and see how the story winds up, shall we?" Dr. Harrison grimaced as he pushed the top six off the table. He opened up the last book and turned to the last page. "I think I know his plan."

"What? How can you understand his notes? You're not an engineer."

"Because he drew a cartoon."

Harrison turned the book towards Agnes. On the page was a childish stick figure of a woman with ridiculously proportioned breasts shooting squiggly lightning bolts out of her hands towards a man with a ridiculous moustache wearing a huge medal and carrying a sword.

"Hc is exhibiting his creation to the Queen today, yes?'

"Yes. There will be an audience of royals, lords, dignitaries and oh, my Lord…."

"Yes, my dear." Harrison closed the book. "I think your uncle plans on using the Galvanized Girl to kill the Kaiser."

"We have to get out of here!" Agnes pulled at Edgar who took a step and then fell to his knees. "What? What's wrong?"

Edgar put his hand inside his vest. "I have a confession to make, darling." He pulled out a bloody rag. "I lied."

"Oh, no! Edgar, you fool! Why didn't you tell me?" Agnes went down to her knees and held him in her lap.

"I'm sorry. I haven't been much help, have I? Just an old man, getting in the way."

"Shut up. You're not old. I'll get you help. Just…just stay here. I'll find a way."

"Yes, my love, go and find a way but not for me. Save the Kaiser."

"To hell with the Kaiser!"

"If I die, what does the world lose? Another pedantic professor. If the Kaiser dies, there will be a war. Thousands will perish. I'm not worth that."

"You are to me. I'll stay here and take care of you!"

"I thought you might say that. Always…always such a stubborn girl." He brushed her hair away from her tear stained face, leaving a bloody smear. "I love you. Agnes. I…I am so sorry…."

He gasped one last time and went still in his beloved's arms.

WINDSOR CASTLE

BY INVITATION OF HER   MOST SACRED MAJESTY

QUEEN VICTORIA

Admit One Person

TO WITNESS THE SPECTACLE OF

THE GALVANIZED GIRL!

THE PARKLAND OF WINDSOR CASTLE

ON WEDNESDAY THE 22ND OF APRIL 1898

CHAPTER SEVEN

Captured Forever

By the command of the Queen, a temporary amphitheater complete with royal blue velvet curtains, arc lamps, and an orchestra pit was constructed on the lush parklands of Windsor Castle. Three stately boxes of seats of different sizes as befitting the occupant's station were built facing the stage for The Queen and her guests. The Royals sat in a gilded, purple velvet curtained box in the center. To the right, in a box painted gold and red with a white cloth cover were seated Lords and Ladies. The lesser nobility sat in the left hand box, painted a pale blue and unshielded from the wind and sun, alongside with the lucky Illustrated Times raffle winners.

The roar of trumpets signaled the arrival of the Queen and everyone scrambled to their assigned seats. Everyone knew it was a curious habit of Her Majesty not to step foot outside her carriage until everyone had been seated.

The Queen, dressed in her usual black mourning wear, was followed closely by Princess Beatrice, her youngest daughter and unofficial secretary, and the Prime Minister, Robert Gascoyne-Cecil, the third Marquis of Salisbury.

Following a few feet behind the Royals were Kaiser Wilhelm II, his chest jingling with military honorific medals. He wore them all to compensate for the one von Bulow forced him to give up to that British brat. Behind him were a pair of his favorite lackeys and swan hunters, General Paul Von Hindenburg, General Erich Ludendorff. On their chests, they were wearing the very ornate silver winged ruby medal from Dr. Pryde. Walking behind the trio, scanning the crowd and nervously rubbing his hands was the State Secretary for Foreign Affairs, Bernard von Bulow.

There was the sound of hissing as the Kaiser's party passed the box of seats.

The Kaiser stopped and, his hand on his sword.

"Who dares-!"

Von Bulow stopped the Kaiser's hand and shook his head; Wilheim snorted out a curse.

"You there! Photographer!" Von Bulow shouted to a man with a camera. "Do you work for the Illustrated Times?"

"Yessir."

"Get to work then! Take a photograph of the Kaiser with the raffle winners and das kinder that is wearing the Kaiser's medal."

"Mein Gott!" Wilheim kicked at the ground, knocking up a divet of grass. "More stroking of this herd?"

Von Bulow gave him a stern look and the Kaiser returned it with a nod and a curt bow.

"Very well, let's get it over with."

The photographer lined the lucky raffle winners up behind the Kaiser and took a last look through the viewscope. He held the rubber bulb high above his head. It was an old photographer's trick to get people to look upwards.

"Yessir, if you would, please, stand there, Kaiser Wilheim. Yes. Thank you. And if you lot would please stand? And, Thomas, stand in the chair so we can see you. Excellent! Now, Thomas, hold up the Kaiser's medal."

The Kaiser watched the sunlight glint off the silver winged medal and clenched his jaw.

The boy held it up high, nearly strangling himself on the blue ribbon. He smiled wide, showing off his missing front two teeth.

"This is the proudest day of my life!" the young boy squealed. "I'll wear it forever!"

"I bet it is, Thomas! Now, three....two...one...SMILE!"

The photographer squeezed the rubber bulb and captured the boy's gap-toothed grin forever.

CHAPTER EIGHT

Behind a Velvet Curtain

Doctor Thaddeus Pryde peeked out from behind the velvet curtains at the audience. His attention was focused on the center box where his prize would be sitting. He recognized his Queen straight away and whispered a heartfelt prayer for her continued good health. He knew the Princess and the Prime Minster from their pictures in the newspaper. The Kaiser was a harder nut to crack. The only renderings Pryde had ever seen were satirical editorial caricatures, much hated by the Queen but loved by the public at large. He was always drawn with an oversized moustache and wearing overlarge military regalia, all of which had been awarded without benefit of any actual military experience. Blood does have its privileges.

"Ah, that has to be him!" Pryde nodded at the tall, barrel chested man sitting next to a poor unfortunate with a withered arm that he hid well from the public but Pryde, with his surgeon's eye for form and function, spotted it quickly. His target had a full beard, true, not just a moustache but he was wearing the medal Pryde had sent the Kaiser and his cronies.

"Excellent. There he is, front row and waiting for destiny." Pryde stroked the black remote activator box he held in his hand. "For Queen and country, let the show commence!"

"It started out like all the other shows. I flew over the crowd, did a few rolls, came back down to the stage, the same old shenanigans. And then the Doc held out a box with a big red button. I never seen that box before, my hand to God. I didn't know.

Doc pushed the button and the hot, silver rush flooded through me again.

"Before, I never had no real different sense 'tween me and the suit. I was just me with a bit more, ya know? Now, the exoskeleton felt alive and alien. Does that make sense?

"My feet left the floor and I was hanging midair. I couldn't do nothing but watch as my palms shot up and towards the crowd. There was a humming, a tingly, ticklish sort of drumming and then bolts of lightning shot out of my hands, zipped through the air and straight into the crowd.

"I was just a puppet, understand. I didn't move my arms, that much I swear! It were the exoskeleton!

"The first one that went down was a boy. He had the medallion in his mouth, sucking on it like a candy. Then, one by one, men went down like dominoes. The Queen's guards did their duty but what good are bullets against lightning? The suit...it picked them off, one by one, like it were shooting cans off a fence.

"I saw them drag Doc away. When they grabbed him, he dropped the box and I fell to the stage, used and empty. Aggie appeared like an angel. She held me and cradled my head. I could see guards rushing towards us, ready to rip us to shreds.

"But I had one more trick up my sleeve."

ILLUSTRATED TIMES, LONDON ISSUE
SPECIAL EDITION
April 1898

ATTEMPTED ASSASINATION AT
WINDSOR CASTLE!!!
'FIREBALLS SHOT OUT FROM HER
HANDS!'

*A young boy's life is snuffed out.
*Galvanized Girl accused.
*Dr. Thaddeus Pryde confined to
Bethleham Royal Hospital.
The Kaiser threatens WAR!

The peace and tranquility of the amphitheater in the parklands of Windsor Castle was violated during the Royal exhibition of The Galvanized Girl.

Witnesses said that during the performance, Dr. Thaddeus Pryce began a rambling, murderous rant and with the push of a button, transformed the beloved Galvanized Girl into an electrical firebomb.

"She looked like an avenging angel, hanging up there in midair." Mrs. George Torrance, a raffle winner, said. "It was a glorious sight. I thought it was part of the show until the bolts shot out, killing the little nipper sitting beside me."

The nipper in question was Thomas Fielding, the nine year old raffle winner. We here at the Illustrated Times, offer our sincere condolences for his loss.

Also killed in the horrific event were Paul von Hindenburg and Erich Ludendorff, generals and dear friends of the Kaiser.

"From our investigations," said Inspector Bernard Franklin of Scotland Yard, "it appears that the lightning bolts were generated from the Galvanized Girl and the bolts targeted each of the medals that were given to the Kaiser and his entourage as gifts by Dr. Thaddeus Pryde. It is a bizarre turn that one of those medals was not on its intended victim."

As readers will remember, little Thomas was given the medal by the Kaiser before the deadly event.

On the subject of Dr. Pryde, Inspector Franklin was very blunt, "Dr. Pryde maintains it was Angels that commanded him to kill the Kaiser to prevent a war or some kind of rot. The poor man had even cut holes in his skull so he could hear them better. He is confined to a cell at Bethlehem Royal Hospital. I suspect he will be a patient there for some time."

Doctors refused to give any official word on his condition but contacts within the hospital confirm that Pryde had horrible wounds in his skull and was stark raving mad. There is little hope for his recovery.

In spite of these condemning facts, the Kaiser refuses to believe it is the work of a lone madman.

"This is an outrage! Who dares strike a blow at Germany?" Wilheim II, Kaiser of Germany, protested. "It is an obvious and blatant attempt by the British to assassinate the leader of the German people and we will not stand for it!"

Bernard Von Bulow, the State Secretary for Foreign Affairs was not available for comment and in conference with Her Majesty's counsel at this time.

As for the whereabouts of the Galvanized Girl, they are, as of this printing, still unknown. Witnesses say that she shot balls of light at guards and ran away with an accomplice. The Illustrated Times has issued a reward of 50 pounds sterling for any information that leads to their capture.

"And there you have it. The whole story. True and simple. I want to set the record straight.

"Since it was you, Illustrated Times, that put a bounty on our heads, it seems only fair that we get a voice.

"So let it be known, to anyone who hears my voice, I'm not a murderer. I'm not a monster. My name is Delilah Ditch. And I never meant to kill nobody, much less start a war.

"But if you come after me and Aggie with any sort of evil intent, there will be one.

"And that's all I have to say."

THE END

ABOUT THE AUTHOR

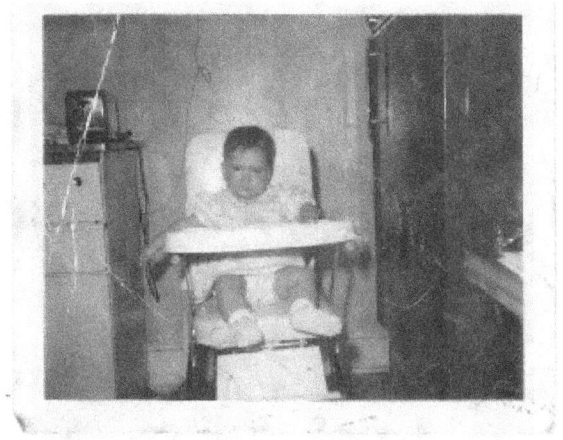

Born with this attitude

Nikki Nelson-Hicks was born in 1965.

It took an entire lifetime to get this weird.

BE CAREFUL WHERE YOU DIG.

There is something very wrong in the Gobi Desert.

"In, The Problem at Gruff Springs, Nikki Nelson-Hicks melds the visceral action of Bone Tomahawk with her own unique brand of pulp horror, offering an exciting new voice for fans of the Weird West genre." – Todd Keisling, *Devil's Creek*

Why do all the women in Poe's life die?
Amy Angler believes she has the answer but
needs one more piece of the puzzle to prove
it.

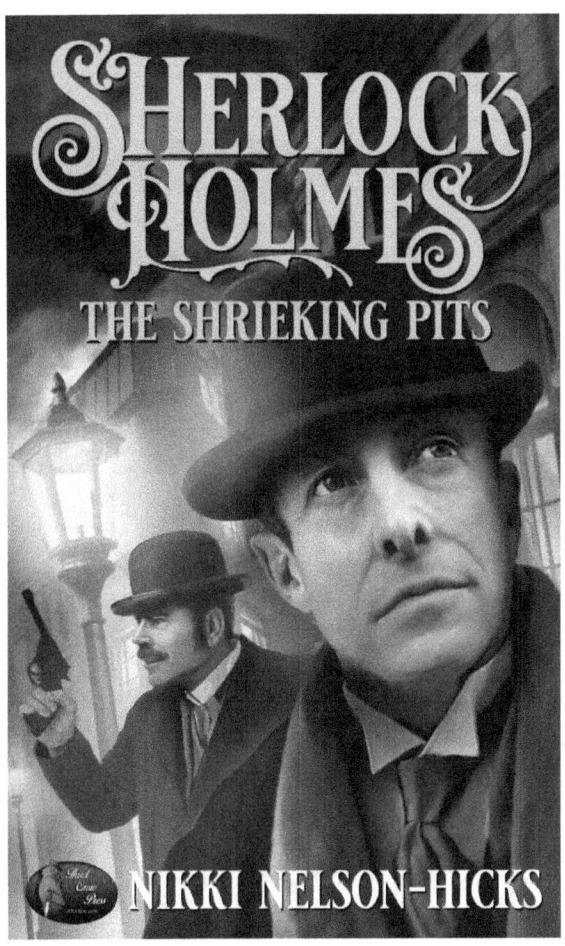

Holmes must use all of his wits to solve the mystery of the Shrieking Pits without adding to the body count.

Two con artists bluff the aristocracy with promises to oust their supernatural squatters. The tables are turned when it turns out that their foe is quite real and the con runs much deeper.

The entire six story saga of the Accidental Detective series with extra vignettes and a teaser for the seventh story:

Silver Screens, Stacks of Gold and a Bloody Nose